The
Princess
and the
Frozen Peas

by Laura North and Joelle Dreidemy

W
FRANKLIN WATTS
LONDON•SYDNEY

This story is based on the traditional fairy tale,
The Princess and the Pea, but with a new twist.
You can read the original story in
Hopscotch Fairy Tales. Can you make
up your own twist for the story?

First published in 2012 by
Franklin Watts
338 Euston Road
London
NW1 3BH

Franklin Watts Australia
Level 17/207 Kent Street
Sydney
NSW 2000

Text © Laura North 2012
Illustrations © Joelle Dreidemy 2012

A CIP catalogue record for this book is available
from the British Library.

ISBN 978 1 4451 0669 4 (hbk)
ISBN 978 1 4451 0675 5 (pbk)

Series Editor: Melanie Palmer
Series Advisor: Catherine Glavina
Series Designer: Peter Scoulding

Printed in China

Franklin Watts is a division of
Hachette Children's Books,
an Hachette UK company
www.hachette.co.uk

There was once a young,
beautiful princess who lived
in a huge kingdom.

One day, a very ugly old King came to the royal palace to marry the princess.

"Oh no," thought the Princess.
"I can't marry him!"

"The King wants proof that she's a real princess before he marries her," said one servant.

"A real princess won't be able to sleep even if there is only a tiny pea underneath a big pile of mattresses," said the other.

GRUMPF
GRUMPF

"I am a real princess," thought the Princess. "But I will pretend that I'm not."

The servants crept into her room and placed a single pea under the pile of mattresses.

"Oh, I am so sleepy," yawned the Princess and pretended to sleep.

The servants watched the Princess. "Look! She's asleep already. The King will be so angry!" cried one.

10

"Maybe one pea wasn't enough," said the other servant. "We must prove that she is a princess!"

The next night, they crept into her
room. "Lots of frozen peas should
do the job!" they whispered.

"Oh, I am so terribly tired!"
said the Princess. She began
snoring loudly.

Next morning, the sun rose early. "What a wonderful night's sleep I've had," the Princess gloated. The servants looked worried.

"But really I've not slept a wink,"
thought the Princess, secretly.

The servants told the King
what had happened.

"What do you mean she's not a
princess?" yelled the King.
"Try harder!"

17

"Let's try other things that start with the letter P," said one servant.

"Good idea," said the other servant.

"That's almost as good as a real pea."

The servants put some
prickly porcupines
into her bed.
But still the
Princess slept.

They tried a pirate ...

and a panda ...

a peacock ...

... and a painter!

ZZZZ^ZZ

But still the Princess slept.

Soon it was the morning of the wedding. "She's not a princess," said the servants to the King. "Call the wedding off," sighed the King, and he left.

"Phew!" said the Princess. She
didn't have to marry the King.
"And now," she said, "I can finally
get a good night's sleep!"

Puzzle 1

Put these pictures in the correct order.
Which event do you think is most important?
Now try writing the story in your own words!

Puzzle 2

1. The King gets very angry.

2. I want to marry a real Princess.

3. I am so sleepy.

4. We must stop her sleeping!

5. I have servants for everything.

6. I cannot marry that ugly King!

Choose the correct speech bubbles for each character. Can you think of any others? Turn over to find the answers.

Answers

Puzzle 1

The correct order is: 1c, 2f, 3d, 4e, 5b, 6a

Puzzle 2

The Princess: 3, 6

The King: 2, 5

The servants: 1, 4